This fun **P** belongs to

_____

Ladybird Reading

Phonics BOOK 4

Contents

A catalogue record for this book is available from the British Library

Published by Ladybird Books Ltd
80 Strand London WC2R 0RL
A Penguin Company

2 4 6 8 10 9 7 5 3 1
© LADYBIRD BOOKS LTD MMVI
LADYBIRD and the device of a Ladybird are trademarks of Ladybird Books Ltd

ISBN-13: 978-1-84646-324-2
ISBN-10: 1-84646-324-6

Printed in Italy

Stunt Duck

by Clive Gifford
illustrated by John Haslam

introducing the **ck** letter group,
as in duck

Stunt Duck gave his
jet pack one last check.

He put the jet pack on his back and locked the straps.

"Stand back,"
said Stunt Duck.

Click! He lit his jet pack with a quick flick.

Stunt Duck shot into the bricks and blocks.

Smack! He struck the
rock at the back.

Crack! Stunt Duck hit the deck. It all went black.

"Nice trick, Stunt Duck, but the film got stuck. Can you do it again?"

Bad luck, Stunt Duck!

Roll up!
Roll up!

by Clive Gifford
illustrated by Charlotte Combe

introducing the **ll** and **ss**
letter groups, as in well and miss

We all had a ball when the fair came to call.

Nell did well
on all the stalls.

Bess won less, but still did well.

The Hall of Chills was full of thrills.

19

I went wild on the
Wacky Wall.

And we sat on the hill as evening fell.

The Sing Song Gang

by Clive Gifford
illustrated by Eric Smith

introducing the **ng** sound,
as in king

DING DONG!
BANG BANG BANG!

"Hang on!" said the King,
as the doorbell rang.

"Open up!
It's the Sing Song Gang!

Would you like us to sing
as you swing on your swing?

You can bang on the gong,

BONG

or play one of the strings."

TWANG

PING

So the gang sang a song,

and the King sang along.

HOW TO USE
Phonics
BOOK 4

This book introduces your child to words including common groups of two or more consonants, such as ng in the word 'king', or ck in the word 'duck'. The fun stories will help your child begin reading simple words containing these consonant groups.

- Read each story through to your child first. Familiarity helps children to identify some of the words and phrases.

- Have fun talking about the sounds and pictures together – what repeated sounds can your child hear in each story?

- Break new words into separate sounds (eg. d-u-ck) and blend their sounds together to say the word.

- Point out how words with the same written ending often rhyme. If k-ing says 'king', what does s-ing or sw-ing say?

32

- Some common words, such as 'one', 'said' and even 'the', can't be read by sounding out. Help your child practise recognising words like these.

Phonic fun

Playing word games is a fun way to build phonic skills. Write down a consonant group and see how many words your child can think of beginning or ending with that group. For extra fun, try making up silly sentences together, using some or all of the words.

The du<u>ck</u> in his so<u>ck</u> gave Mi<u>ck</u> a sho<u>ck</u>.

Ladybird Reading

Phonics

Phonics is part of the Ladybird Reading range. It can be used alongside any other reading programme, and is an ideal way to practise the reading work that your child is doing, or about to do in school.

Ladybird has been a leading publisher of reading programmes for the last fifty years. **Phonics** combines this experience with the latest research to provide a rapid route to reading success.

The fresh quirky stories in Ladybird's twelve **Phonics** storybooks are designed to help your child have fun learning the relationship between letters, or groups of letters, and the sounds they represent.

This is an important step towards independent reading – it will enable your child to tackle new words by sounding out and blending their separate parts.

How Phonics works

- The stories and rhymes introduce the most common spellings of over 40 key sounds, known as phonemes, in a step-by-step way.

- Rhyme and alliteration (the repetition of an initial sound) help to emphasise new sounds.

- Bright amusing illustrations provide helpful picture clues and extra appeal.